I AM
SAMMY,
TRUSTED GUIDE

I AM
SAMMY,
TRUSTED GUIDE

Catherine Stier

illustrated by
Francesca Rosa

Albert Whitman & Company
Chicago, Illinois

In memory of my loving and much-loved mom,
Barbara Beadle, who collected
and cherished stories and books—CS

To my loving parents, Michele and Germana;
thank you for guiding me on my journey.—FR

Library of Congress Cataloging-in-Publication data
is on file with the publisher.
Text copyright © 2020 by Catherine Stier
Illustrations copyright © 2020 by Albert Whitman & Company
Illustrations by Francesca Rosa
First published in the United States of America
in 2020 by Albert Whitman & Company
ISBN 978-0-8075-1672-0 (hardcover)
ISBN 978-0-8075-1675-1 (ebook)

Printed in the United States of America
10 9 8 7 6 5 4 3 2 1 LB 24 23 22 21 20

Design by Rick DeMonico

For more information about Albert Whitman & Company,
visit our website at www.albertwhitman.com.

Contents

Chapter 1

Car Trouble

One thing I've learned about Chicago—it is one lively city! Crowds hurry by, lights flash, horns honk. And the smells! Some can be hard for a dog like me to resist.

Like right now, I'm walking with Jessie past a food stand. The yummy scent of bacon and sausage almost stops me in my tracks!

Oh pup, that smells good! I think.

Still, I have a job to do. If I let myself get

distracted by those delicious breakfast smells even for a moment, there could be trouble.

We come to a street curb, and I sit. That's how I let Jessie know about the curb, so she doesn't stumble. With a backward movement of her foot, Jessie tells me that she gets my message: *Warning! Curb ahead!*

Jessie and I are a team. She's my person, and I'm her guide dog. Jessie is a freshman—a first-year student—at a university. She's blind, which means she can't see the way some other people can. When we walk together, Jessie holds a handle attached to my harness with her left hand. I help her stay safe as she moves from place to place.

As we turn a corner, a frisky puppy bounds down the sidewalk toward us. He pulls on his leash and gives a little yap. This pup wants to play—I can see that.

Still, I stay on course and walk right past him.

Not now, little one, I think. *I'm doing important work.*

But that spunky little guy reminds me of my own puppy days.

I was just a pup cuddled up with my mama and my littermates when I heard the first hints about my future.

"I wonder which of you has what it takes to become a guide dog," a trainer said when she came to check on us.

I didn't pay much attention to her words. Back then, I only thought about snuggling, sleeping, eating, and playing. My littermates and I were golden retrievers like our mama, with fuzzy golden fur and floppy ears. Our names all started with the same sound too. There were my siblings, Sherlock, Stetson, Sally, and Sierra, and me, Sammy. It could be confusing at times!

When we grew a little older, the trainers planned fun things for us. We played in a little

ball pit and slid down tiny slides. We met other dogs and our first cat, bunny, and even a friendly baby goat. We were coaxed to walk up a ramp or through a little tunnel—and got lots of praise when we did.

I guess they wanted us to be ready for anything and everything!

I hope I am.

Today, as Jessie and I walk along on this bright fall morning, I spot a hazard ahead.

Uh-oh.

There's a motor scooter parked on the sidewalk blocking our way. Quickly, I veer left, steering around it. Through the handle she holds, Jessie can feel my movement. She knows to move left too.

I'm glad Jessie trusts me enough to follow my lead.

Truth is, the two of us are still getting to know each other. We haven't been a team for very long.

When I first met Jessie, she used a long cane to help her get around. She'd never had a guide dog, and I was new to my job. We have been working now with a trainer, Elena, to help us understand each other.

"Leaving the cane at home and putting faith in your dog isn't easy at first," Elena said when she introduced us.

And not every dog is cut out for this job. I'm proud to be a guide dog, but I worry too. After all my training and testing, I *really* want to get this right.

As we near the university campus, I startle a bit at the sound of flapping wings. I watch a pigeon land not far away. Some dogs might give chase to that city bird. But I only allow myself a quick glance while we cruise by.

When I turn my head forward again, though, I tense up. There's a careless driver speeding down the road. I see the car's front wheels begin to swerve into the parking garage entrance right in front of us! I step back and stop. Jessie can't see the car. She doesn't know why I've stopped, so she urges me on.

"Forward," she says.

But I ignore the command.

"Forward," she says again.

I don't move.

This is the trickiest part of my job. I've been trained to keep Jessie safe by doing the things she says—unless following the command will lead to danger.

Elena, the trainer, calls this intelligent

disobedience. "It takes a really smart and confident dog to know when to follow a command and when to ignore it," she explained once.

At the sound of squealing tires turning right in front of us, Jessie gasps and steps back. She knows now why I stopped. She knows, too,

what could have happened if we had moved forward. I can hear Jessie's shaky breath. Then she leans close.

"Good dog, Sammy. Smart dog! That was a close call!" She scratches my right shoulder. Already Jessie knows that's my favoritest place in the world for a scratch!

I'm glad Jessie is happy with me. What just happened, though, is another reminder—I *always* have to focus on the job.

After all, Jessie is counting on me.

Chapter 2
Working and Waiting

When we finally reach the university, there are even more sights, sounds, and smells. Students have set up colorful tables with bright banners. They call out to other students passing by.

"Buy a sweet cupcake to support the Honor Society!"

"Register to vote!"

"Join the Women in Science Club!"

"Sign up to study overseas!"

I hear a clattering noise close by.

Uh-oh. What's that?

But it's only a guy gliding by on a skateboard.

"Isn't it exciting to be on campus, Sammy?" Jessie says happily. "There's so much going on!"

As we near a familiar building, Jessie says, "Find the door," and I go to the entrance. Inside, we head for a classroom where a group of students are talking. Some greet Jessie as I lead her to a seat.

Soon, a man carrying a brown case walks in. "Good morning, professor," one of the students says. I settle near Jessie's feet as the professor begins to speak. Jessie records what he says on her phone and takes notes with a special device.

From my spot on the floor, I can smell a yummy peanut-butter sandwich stuffed inside a nearby backpack. Up ahead, I spot a crumpled chip bag I wouldn't mind sniffing. The professor is in front of the class, pointing to a chart with a stick.

That scrawny stick isn't as good as a tree branch, but I could still play fetch with it, I think.

But I'm at work, and I'm in a classroom, so I resist these temptations. After all, I learned how to behave in class a while ago, with my other human family, the Robinsons.

I met the Robinsons when I was just eight weeks old. "Sammy, your volunteer puppy raisers are here!" a trainer at the guide dog facility had said one morning.

And there, in the next room, were the Robinsons—Dad, a little boy named Marcus, and a taller boy, Jayden. I was so excited! I

greeted my new puppy raisers with a wagging tail and kisses. Then they took me on a long car ride and brought me to live in their house.

The Robinsons were the ones who taught me my first simple commands. I learned *sit*, *stand*, and *down*.

And we did fun things together! It took me a while to get used to the idea of wearing a guide-dog-in-training vest. But when I did, I was allowed to go inside places other dogs couldn't, like the library, the yogurt shop, and even the grocery store.

One summer's day, we went someplace extra-special.

"It will be a good experience for Sammy to come to the celebration," Dad said. "He should get used to crowds."

We walked to something called a carnival. I'd

never seen so many people in one place! Some carried around giant stuffed animals, while others held apples on a stick. Jayden munched on a pink cloud he called cotton candy.

"Dad, can we ride the Ferris wheel?" I heard Marcus ask. Then I stayed with Dad as Marcus and Jayden went up, up, up on some big, creaking machine.

Hey, you two, where are you going? Is that safe? I thought. *Get back down here with me!*

That night, we all sat on a blanket in a grassy spot near the carnival. Suddenly, bright lights exploded in the sky! Loud bangs filled the air too. I jumped to my feet and howled and barked and pulled on my leash.

That sounds like danger! I thought. *I must protect my family!*

But Marcus patted me and spoke soft words.

"It's okay, Sammy. Those noises used to scare me too! But it's just part of the celebration."

Humans have a strange way of celebrating! I thought. But once I knew everything was okay, I stayed calm for the rest of the show.

"We can note in Sammy's monthly training report that he's comfortable with crowds. He does pretty well with Fourth of July fireworks too," Dad said when the lights and banging stopped. "That's a good sign."

The tall boy, Jayden, was the one who brought me to my first classroom. I went with him to his high school. I wore my vest, but everyone was so excited, Jayden had to remind them not to pet me, since I was training.

I remember that in one classroom, there were funny smells as the big kids mixed liquids from skinny glass tubes. In another, the scents of paint and clay filled the room—and all the students drew pictures of me!

I wasn't working with Jayden as a guide dog, but going to his school did teach me how to act around lots of people. The most important thing I learned was how to wait to do certain things. During class breaks, Jayden would bring me to the same outdoor spot. "Okay, Sammy, do your business," he'd say. And so I would.

Sometimes, I went with Jayden after school

to the gym for something he called "basketball practice." Practice looked more like playtime to me! Everyone ran and jumped and scampered about—just like I do during *my* playtime!

But my own playtime always came later, when we got home. Jayden would pull off my vest, and we would play catch in the backyard. Jayden would toss a toy into the air, and I'd jump up and grab it again and again until we were both dog-tired.

As the professor in Jessie's class continues to talk and point with that stick, these happy memories of the Robinsons make me sigh.

If I show that I am a good guide dog, my new life will be with Jessie. I love Jessie. We're a team, after all, and I want to do my absolute best for her. But so far, getting used to working with Jessie and living in this new place has been challenging, with lots of new things to learn.

I admit that sometimes I think back to those games of catch with Jayden or snuggles and quiet talks with Marcus. Along with really wanting to prove myself in my new career, I guess I'm missing the Robinsons a bit too.

Chapter 3
Practice Makes Perfect

"You must be excited!" Elena the trainer says when she meets us after class. "Tonight's the big night!"

I look up at Jessie and tilt my head. *What's happening tonight?* I wonder.

"Yes, I'm very excited about the concert," says Jessie. "This will be my first ever solo. Thank you for meeting me here at the theater."

"Of course! A solo with the university's top choir is a huge honor."

"Thanks," Jessie says. "I'm so glad I joined the Pop Notes."

The Pop Notes? I think. *I know about them.*

The first time Jessie told me we were going to a Pop Notes practice, I expected it to be like Jayden's basketball practice. Instead, we walked into a small classroom.

Where are all the bouncing balls? And the people running around? I wondered. All I saw

that afternoon was a group of students singing.

I wasn't disappointed for long though. After a while, I liked what I heard! I may not know much about human music, but the sound of those students' voices blending together made my tail thump!

And tonight is the Pop Notes concert.

Oh pup, I've never been to a concert before—whatever that is!

"How can we help you get ready for tonight's performance?" Elena asks Jessie.

"The Pop Notes director wants us to do something special," Jessie says. "Once the audience is seated, we'll start the show. We'll walk from the back of the theater down the side aisles, singing as we climb the stairs to the stage."

"That sounds lovely," says Elena.

"Yes, but we've only practiced in the choir room because the theater is always being used for other student events," Jessie explains. "I'm allowed in for a few minutes now with you and Sammy to check things out."

"Let's go inside then," Elena says.

When we step into the theater, I see it's a really big place with a high ceiling, like Jayden's school gym. But it's very different! There's a large wooden floor up front, but it's not like the basketball court. It's raised, with thick curtains on each side. There are lots of chairs in this place. Each looks as cushy as a doggy bed, and much more comfy than the gym's metal bleachers.

"Let's practice getting you on that stage," Elena says to Jessie.

Jessie takes a deep breath.

"Just remember what we've talked about,

Jessie," Elena says with a kind voice. "Trust your dog."

"Okay. Here goes," Jessie says.

From the back of the theater, Jessie and I walk down the aisle. When we reach the front, I put my paws on the bottom stair. Through the handle, Jessie feels me step up. This lets her know that we've reached a staircase. Jessie pats me on the head and puts one hand on the rail. Up we go till we reach the big wooden stage.

We've got this! I think.

Then comes the tricky part. Jessie moves, with me at her side, to a little mat in front of a microphone. The mat marks the center of the stage, and Jessie can feel the different material through her shoes. Once Jessie finds the mat, we stand there a moment, facing row after row of seats.

"Perfect!" Elena says.

Still, we practice this a few more times. I understand why. Whatever is going to happen at that concert tonight, I can tell it is a big deal for Jessie. She doesn't want anything to go wrong.

"Do you feel confident about getting to the stage now?" Elena asks after our last run-through.

"I do," Jessie says. "But I know it will be different tonight when there's an audience full of people watching me."

"You'll do great," Elena assures her. "And I'll be one of those people in that audience, cheering you on!"

I'll be here for you, too, Jessie! I think. *Don't forget that!*

"I believe our work here is done," Elena says cheerily. And then her voice turns more serious. "So, Jessie, after four weeks, this is our last day training together. How do you feel about that?"

Jessie smiles. "You've been great, Elena, and I've learned so much! Sammy is wonderful too. Now I'm so excited about all my plans for the future. You know, pursuing my business degree. Starting my career someday. Traveling. Continuing with my singing too."

"I'm glad to hear it," says Elena.

"But I do have one question," Jessie says, and pauses. "Do *you* think Sammy and I are ready to be on our own?"

I see Elena smile. "I've watched as you two have bonded over time. You and Sammy work together safely and effectively as a team," she says. "And if I have one last bit of advice, it's what I've told you before."

"I know," says Jessie. "Trust my dog."

"That's right," Elena says. "Trust your dog. Trust Sammy."

Chapter 4

A Strange Smell

After Elena says goodbye, Jessie and I leave campus. We walk along the city sidewalks until we reach a place with good smells drifting out through the door. A lady sits at one of the outdoor tables, sipping coffee with a poodle resting near her.

"Skippy, lie down," the lady says when her dog jumps and yips at the sight of me.

Most dogs, like Skippy, aren't allowed inside this café. But most dogs aren't working, like me.

We are just about to go inside the café when I see a young woman hurrying down the street toward us.

Hey, I know her! That's Jessie's friend Mei! I think.

By the time Mei reaches us, she's out of breath.

"Oh, Jessie, I'm so sorry," Mei says. "I know we were supposed to meet at one o'clock. Am I late? Did I keep you waiting?"

Jessie laughs. "No, Mei, I'm early! When I used the cane to get around, things were much slower. I have to remember now that with Sammy, I can zip to places in no time."

"Whew!" says Mei. "Good. Now let's get some lunch! I don't have much time before my next class. And we have a lot to talk about."

The three of us walk into the café, and the woman at the front counter gives me a quick glance. "Sorry, miss, no dogs allowed..." Then she sees my harness and handle. "Oh, I apologize!" she says. "Of course your guide dog is welcome."

The woman shows us to a table.

Jessie says the command "tuck," and I scoot myself under the table.

As soon as we're settled, Mei begins talking in an excited voice.

"So have you told your parents yet? That you want to live in the dorms next semester?" Mei asks.

"I did. You too?" Jessie says.

"Yep," Mei says.

"What did they say?"

Mei sighs. "They say they'll miss me living at home. But they know that moving onto campus is an important step for me."

"Mine said the same thing!" Jessie says.

"So we're doing this? We're going to be college roommates? You, me, and Sammy?" Mei asks.

I raise my head at the sound of my name.

Wait, what?

These two have something in the works that includes me—I can tell!

"I guess we're doing this!" Jessie says happily.

"Yes!" Mei says, clapping her hands. "Oh, we'll have to go shopping for dorm stuff soon!"

While Jessie and Mei munch on salads and sandwiches above me, I settle back down.

After a while, Mei pops up from her seat.

"I better be going," she says. "I'll be late for class if I don't hurry. Bye, Jessie! Sing sweet as a songbird at the concert tonight!"

Jessie laughs. "Will do. Good luck in class," she says. "I'm going to stay here and work on homework for a bit."

It isn't long after Mei leaves that something new catches my attention.

There are always lots of smells in this café—soap, sweat, perfume, and deodorant from the customers and servers. There's the scent of coffee, tea, and all the good aromas from the meals on the table. But now I sense another unusual and heavy smell that seems to be drifting over from the cooking area.

I raise my nose to check out this strange scent.

Something's not right, I think.

Suddenly there's the sound of running feet.
A man in an apron rushes into the dining area.

"Attention, everyone!" he yells. "There's a
fire in the kitchen. For your safety, please exit
the café—now!"

Chapter 5
A Dog's Decision

Plates and silverware clatter as people at the other tables scramble from their seats.

Jessie jumps up and grabs my handle. She turns toward the door we came in. "Go right, Sammy. Find the door," she says.

But the front door she is stepping toward is not far from the kitchen. Smoke begins to pour from the kitchen entrance. A gray, moving cloud billows toward where we came in.

Should we go in that direction? Or is there a safer way out?

No one taught me about smoke or fire during my training. But I have my instincts. I know I have to think fast. The heavy smell is growing stronger. That fire could be spreading quickly.

I make the decision to disobey Jessie's command.

There's another door, on the other side of the café, away from the smoke. Some customers are headed that way.

So that's the direction I turn to.

"Are you sure, Sammy? Very sure?" Jessie asks nervously when I move to the left. Then I hear her repeat the words Elena has told her to remember: "Trust my dog," Jessie whispers to herself. "Trust Sammy."

We move quickly past tables full of half-eaten meals. I guide Jessie around a chair someone tipped over in the rush to get out. Many of the servers and cooks are hurrying right behind us.

Jessie lets me lead her safely to the other door. We burst through the exit and find ourselves outside in the bright fall sunshine and cool, fresh air.

I look back and see more smoke filling the restaurant.

I'm glad we got out in time!

Chapter 6
Passing the Test

"Mom, I'm okay," Jessie says. Her voice sounds calm on the phone, but her hand on my handle shakes a bit. Big trucks with loud sirens race this way down the street.

"There was a kitchen fire in the café where I was studying." Jessie speaks louder to be heard over the street noises. "But we're all right. Sammy led me out!"

"Yes, Sammy is a good dog," Jessie continues. "Yes, I'm fine. No, no one was hurt. We all got out fast, the customers and the café staff. The fire department just arrived. I'm heading to the bus stop," she says. "I'll be home soon. Love ya, Mom."

"Well, Sammy, that's twice you've kept me safe today!" Jessie says when she puts her phone away. She scratches my shoulder. "Now, let's go home."

We begin walking the familiar route to the bus stop. As we get close to the street corner, we slow down. There are raised bumps at the corner that Jessie can feel beneath her shoes. That lets her know the street is just ahead.

"Find the button," Jessie says. I lead her to a pole with a big metal button. I place my nose under the button, and Jessie reaches for my

head. She slides her hand along my upturned snout until her fingers rest on the button. It tickles me a bit!

After Jessie presses the button, an electronic voice gives the warning: "Wait! Wait! Wait!" And we do.

When it's finally safe to cross, a special tone sounds from the speaker.

I admit I was a bit confused the first time I came upon a talking traffic pole. That voice seemed to come from nowhere!

Who's that? Where are you? I thought. But I'm used to it now.

Once we cross the street, Jessie gives the command, "Find a seat," and I lead her to the empty bench at the bus stop.

As we wait for the bus, Jessie makes another phone call. "You'll never guess what happened, Elena," she says. I hear Jessie tell Elena all about the fire in the café. "Sammy wouldn't let me move toward the smoke. Not only is Sammy smart, but he's full of courage too," she says.

Courage? I think. *Hey, I've heard that word before.*

With no sign of the bus yet, I begin to think back to the time when I was about a year and a half old. I was starting advanced training, or doggy college, as Jayden called it. And it was time to leave the Robinsons.

When they brought me back to the guide dog facility, Marcus cried and Jayden got quiet.

Dad spoke gently to his sons that day. "It takes a lot of love and courage to tell someone goodbye as they leave for the next, exciting step in their life," Dad said. "But you can be proud of all you have done to get Sammy ready for his new adventure. He's going to change someone's life."

The two boys nodded then.

"Have fun at doggy college," Jayden said with one last hug. "I think you have a lot of courage too, Sammy."

I looked back one last time at the Robinsons as a trainer led me away.

I admit, it was hard to leave them behind.

Still, I was never lonely or bored at the guide dog campus. Jayden was right—I was at doggy college, and I had a lot to learn!

I was one of four dogs that Elena trained one-on-one. At other times, she worked with my sister Sierra, and two yellow Labrador siblings, Dory and Duncan.

At first, Elena and I practiced some of the same commands that the Robinsons had taught me, like *sit* and *stand* and *down*. Soon, we began working on new things during our morning and afternoon training sessions. I learned to walk in a straight line around the facility grounds, which is more difficult than you'd think! It turns out, most dogs and humans

tend to veer one way or the other when they walk.

I was taught to sit at curbs and at the top of stairs, and I got used to the feeling of wearing a harness and a handle. Elena showed me that I needed to be aware of overhead dangers as well. I may be able to pass under a low-hanging sign, but humans are a lot taller than dogs. If I walked straight ahead, the person with me might run smack into that sign!

During training, I also learned about that tricky thing Elena calls intelligent disobedience. When I ignored a command to go forward into busy traffic, I was praised!

Later, Elena and I often left the guide dog grounds to train in unfamiliar areas. Once, we even went someplace called an airport.

This is as busy as the Fourth of July carnival! I thought once we got inside the huge building.

Lots of people hurried around, carrying bags or pulling suitcases behind them. We boarded a big metal airplane, and I calmly lay on the rumbling floor by Elena's feet for the whole flight. That tickled my tummy a bit! When we landed, Elena gave me fresh water and took me to do my business outside. Then we got right back on another plane!

"I can report that Sammy aced the plane

trip!" Elena said when we returned to the guide dog facility later that afternoon. "He'll be a good match for someone who wants to travel."

For my final tests, Elena wore a blindfold and held my handle as another trainer walked close by us. The three of us strolled down neighborhood sidewalks, through train stations, and along busy city streets. I did well enough on those blindfold tests that Elena knew I was

ready to be matched with a person.

But not every dog on Elena's training team got to be a guide dog.

"Dory is going to be career changed," I heard Elena tell another trainer. "She's letting us know that being a guide dog is not the job for her. She's not as high energy as some dogs, but she's very gentle and loving. I think she'll make a great therapy dog or maybe a diabetic alert dog," Elena said. "I have a few people in mind who I know would like to adopt her."

That's when I first learned that there are lots of different jobs a dog can do!

Even so, I know now that I've found my calling. Being a guide dog is what I want most, even if it does take a lot of training and a bit of courage.

Suddenly, I hear a rumbling motor and turn to see the bus pulling up. Jessie stands up beside me. Time to do the work I've been trained to do!

Chapter 7

Unexpected Stop

On the bus, a little girl sits near us, looking at me. She begins to reach out to pet me when a woman's voice stops her. "No, London, honey, that's a guide dog. He's working."

The girl pulls her hand back.

"Miss," the little girl, London, says to Jessie. "Does your dog really work?"

"Oh, yes," says Jessie. "Sammy here has a

very important job. I can't see, so he helps me get around."

"You can't see anything?" London asks.

"That's right. I've been blind since I was born," Jessie says.

"Oh," the little girls says. She stares at me some more.

"Does Sammy always have to work?" she asks.

Jessie's voice is cheerful. "No, not all the time. He likes to play like any other dog. One of his favorite games is hide-and-seek. I'll hide in the house and call him, and when he finds me, I tell him what a good dog he is."

"Hide-and-seek is one of my favorite games too!" London says. "Sammy must be a fun doggy."

"Lots of fun. Smart too," Jessie says.

Aw, how nice! Jessie's bragging about me, I think.

Just then the bus driver pulls over and stops. He turns to us passengers to make an announcement.

"Sorry, folks. I won't be stopping at Willow Street. There's a detour due to sewer work, and I can't get there. We're being routed to another stop around the block. I apologize, miss," the bus driver says to Jessie. "I know that Willow Street is your usual stop."

"Thank you," says Jessie. "But no worries."

"Can your dog find your way back to Willow Street?" London's mother asks.

"No, actually, he can't. Sammy is a smart dog, but I have to tell him which way to go," says Jessie. "It's not a problem, though. The driver said we'll be just around the block from the stop. As long as the sidewalk is still open, I can find my way."

"Oh, okay," says the woman. "But if you need any help, let us know. That's our stop too."

The bus slows to a stop, and Jessie and I get up. The friendly bus driver gives Jessie directions, and she thanks him.

Jessie gives the command "Right," and I turn right.

As we walk away, I hear London's voice, full of surprise.

"Mommy, that doggy knows right and left,

like I just learned!"

"Yes, he does, London," says the woman. "I'm as impressed as you are!"

As we walk this new route, I see a big tree glowing with fall colors by the sidewalk. But there's a problem. One branch is hanging too low. It's no trouble for a dog like me to pass under, but if Jessie keeps walking, it could hurt her. I steer left and move us to the edge of the sidewalk so she misses the branch, just as I was trained to do. Then I curve around back to the center.

Now, up ahead, we have to cross another street—but this one doesn't have a traffic light or a button to push. Jessie stops to listen for the traffic instead. When she hears it's safe, she gives the command, "Forward."

"Left," says Jessie once we are across. And

there it is, just a few steps away! I recognize the Willow Street bus stop!

"Find a seat," Jessie says, and I quickly lead her to the bus stop.

She reaches a hand out to touch it and smiles.

"This is our usual bus stop. We know our way home from here! We did it, Sammy!" she says.

Yes we did, I think.

Is there anything Jessie and I can't do?

Chapter 8

Finally Home

Back at home, Jessie removes my handle and harness and brings me to the backyard. She and I have been so busy, we haven't had much playtime today. So right away I begin bounding about, frisky as a pup.

Jessie lowers herself to the ground and laughs. "Sammy, you're a different dog when the harness comes off, aren't you?"

Oh pup, you bet I am!

Now that I'm off duty, I don't worry about avoiding distractions. If there's a smell I want to explore, I chase it down. If something tempts me, like that big pile of leaves Jessie's dad raked, I dive right in!

It's while I'm rolling in the crackling leaves that Jessie calls me over.

"Elena told me about a game you played with your puppy raisers, Sammy," she says. Then Jessie pulls a new toy from her jacket pocket.

I remember Jayden and I played catch with a toy just like that. But will Jessie know how it's done?

Jessie stands, winds up, and tosses the toy into the sky.

Hey, you do know what to do, Jessie! I think. *And you've got a pretty good arm!*

"Catch it, Sammy!" she says. I spring up on my hind legs and grab that toy right out of the air!

Then I run over and drop it at Jessie's feet. She tosses it, and I jump to get it again and again.

I'm so happy you like catch, too, Jessie! I think. *This is my favoritest game ever!*

When I'm worn out from all the fun, I come back and sit next to Jessie to catch my breath. She sits, too, and puts her arm around me. We stay that way for a moment.

"Can I tell you something, Sammy?" Jessie says quietly. "Not as my guide, but as my friend?"

I settle close to her. I remember that Marcus's voice always got quiet and serious, like Jessie's is now, when he had big feelings to sort out.

"There's so much on my mind right now," Jessie says. "Like, I wonder if you and I are really ready to be on our own, without Elena. What do you think? Can we do this, Sammy?"

Jessie pauses. I can tell she has more to say.

"Also, I haven't told anyone this, but I'm nervous about the Pop Notes concert tonight. Not about getting to the stage. I trust you for that, Sammy. I'm getting butterflies in my stomach at the thought of singing by myself in front of all those people."

Butterflies in your tummy? Yuck! I think. I lean over and lick her face, and Jessie laughs.

"That's right, Sammy. I won't be by myself, will I? You'll be right there next to me. But what if I miss a note? Or forget the words?"

I won't mind, Jessie.

"And something else is bothering me, Sammy. Something I'm not ready to talk to Mei or my parents about yet. It's this…Part of me can't wait to move into the dorms next semester. I mean, who wouldn't want to be roommates with her best friend and a great dog like you?

60

But part of me is not sure I can do it. It's a big change for me. I worry I'll get homesick."

I duck my head under Jessie's hand. I hope that being here together while Jessie pets my head will help her feel calm. I know it worked wonders when Marcus had worries.

"You see, Sammy," Jessie continues, "we humans—well, sometimes we have to move from what's safe and familiar to accomplish important things."

Jessie pats my head.

"It isn't always easy," she continues. "Sometimes we even have to be brave enough to leave home to find our future, you know?"

Then she catches her breath like she's just realized something.

"But of course you do know that, don't you, Sammy? That's exactly what you've done, and that's what brought you to me!"

Jessie leans over and hugs me again.

"Sammy," Jessie says gently, "I haven't told you this yet, but thank you. Thank you for all the time you've spent learning and training to become my guide dog. If there's anything I'm sure of right now, it's this: I'm so glad you're here with me."

Jessie scratches me in my very favorite spot on my shoulder.

I'm glad we're together, too, Jessie, I think.

And for the first time since I've met her, I feel like I've found a true home here with Jessie.

Chapter 9

A Brave Moment

In the evening, Jessie's parents drop us off by the university's theater. As we head toward the entrance, I sense Jessie's uneasiness. Maybe I'm a little jumpy too. She takes a deep breath and smiles as we enter a room where the Pop Notes have gathered. Everyone in the room wears fancy dresses or suits with bow ties. I'm looking spiffy in a bow tie too.

"Ready for our vocal warm-ups?" the student director asks.

The group begins singing, their voices starting low and going higher and higher.

If I wasn't on duty, I might howl along too! I think.

The warm-ups go on for a while until someone calls out, "Okay, everyone. It's showtime!"

Jessie and I and the Pop Note members leave the practice room and head to the back of the theater.

This is it, I know. Jessie's big moment. She trusts me to get her to the stage.

I sure don't want to mess this up, I think. Even though we practiced, things are different tonight. The theater is darker and noisier. It's crammed with people. Some are turning around to stare.

The director plays a sound on a small instrument. That's the signal! The group slowly moves down the aisle on each side of the audience, singing as they go. Jessie and I are last in line, waiting our turn to move forward.

When Jessie hears the footsteps of the woman in front of us, she quietly gives the "forward" command, and we start walking too. The theater is alive with the pretty, lively sounds of all the Pop Notes' voices joining together.

The people in the seats turn to watch us walk

by. Some little kids wave. I try to stay focused and don't turn to look. We pass people I know. Elena is in the audience, and Mei too! But I don't stop to greet them either. I lead Jessie to the side of the stage. I put my feet on the bottom stair to warn her and keep her from stumbling.

Jessie feels the movement of the handle and knows what that means. She pats me, and we climb the stairs to the stage.

Whew! So far, so good.

With the rest of the choir along each side of the stage, Jessie and I move forward. She finds her place on the small mat in the center of the stage and stops before the microphone.

We did it! I think. We're at the right place at the right moment. I've done my part. The rest is up to Jessie.

The other singers lower their voices to a hum. I feel Jessie's hand tremble a little on my handle. A bright light shines on the two of us. Then Jessie's voice rises, sweet and clear, and pours out into the theater. I stand beside her, facing a crowd of smiling faces as she sings. The words seem to come straight from her heart:

Stepping out onto this journey,
I am braver than you know.

Some people nod their heads to the rhythm of the song. I see Mei rub her arms like humans do when they are cold. But it's not chilly in here at all!

Jessie's mom and dad are in the front row, and both have tears in their eyes.

When the song ends, people clap so hard it sounds like thunder rumbling through the theater. Jessie bows, then moves back with me to a place among the other Pop Notes. I look up, and I see Jessie's wide smile.

Way to go, Jessie!

I am so proud of her, and a little proud of myself too. I'm beginning to think that together, Jessie and I really can do anything.

Chapter 10

A Very Special Day

"It's your special day, Sammy," Jessie says the next morning as we load into the car with her parents.

I don't know what's special about today, I think. *But I do love a car ride!*

When the car finally stops, I recognize the place right away. We are at the guide dog facility!

We all unload and head toward an outdoor

table. On the way, my nose twitches. There's a familiar human scent in the air. As we move forward, it hits me.

Hey, I know those people behind the table!

I'm wearing my harness, and I'm on duty, but I can't help myself. My whole body quivers as we draw near the volunteers handing out name tags.

It's Dad! And Jayden! And Marcus too.

"Sammy," Jayden says. "Is that you?"

Yes, it's me!

I'm all wiggles and whines now, I'm so excited.

"We were Sammy's puppy raisers," Dad explains to Jessie and her family.

"Oh!" Jessie says with a laugh. "No wonder he's acting this way. Please, then, you must say hi to Sammy."

Dad, Marcus, and Jayden come around the table. I'm so happy I could bust!

"I missed you so much, Sammy," Marcus says.

Dad just says, "Well, well, well. How are you doing, Sammy?"

Jayden stoops close to me. "You made it, buddy. You're a certified guide dog. I am so proud of you," he says.

After that, Jessie, her parents, and the Robinsons shake hands and introduce themselves.

"We can't wait to see you both honored at Sammy's graduation today," Dad tells Jessie.

So that's why today is special, I think. *It's my graduation day!*

I've been to a guide dog graduation before. But I've never been the one graduating!

I get one last snuggle from Marcus before Jessie, her parents, and I head to the outdoor pavilion.

The pavilion fills with people and dogs. Colorful balloons brighten a podium up front. Jessie and her family settle into seats near people I know.

Oh pup, Elena and Mei are here too! I think happily as I tuck myself close to Jessie's feet.

Everyone chats together, but quiets when a woman speaks from the podium.

"I'm Leila Campos, president of our guide dog organization. We have a lot of pups and people to honor as we celebrate our guide dog graduates and our other dogs' milestones today!" she says.

First she calls up several puppies with their new puppy raisers.

"Would the Patel family and Molly please step forward," the speaker says. A young Labrador with a shiny yellow coat bounds up with her new family. "Molly is curious, energetic, and loving," the speaker says. "Her new puppy raisers are the Patel family, who will place her training vest on her today."

A teen girl leans down to fit the blue fabric vest on the pup and gets a lick on the face!

Two more puppies receive their vests too.

Hey, pups, have fun with your new people!
I think.

"Next are the dogs who are leaving their puppy raisers' homes to start advanced training," the speaker says. "Their training vest will be replaced by the harness they have earned."

"As these dogs come up, we will honor their puppy raisers too," the speaker continues. "Our awesome volunteer puppy raisers welcome these young dogs into their homes. They spend twelve to eighteen months helping prepare and socialize the future guide dogs that will change people's lives. We honor and thank our puppy raisers with this trophy." The speaker holds up something gold and shiny.

I remember when the Robinsons got that trophy! I think. *It has a statue of a dog on top!*

After several more dogs and people come up, the speaker pauses.

"Finally, the big moment," she says. "We celebrate the graduation and certification of our newest guide dogs. And we introduce our clients with visual impairments who have been partnered with these dogs. Let me tell you, these are some incredible, unstoppable teams!"

There are whoops, hand clapping, and even a little foot stomping.

"That's us, Sammy," Jessie whispers. "An

unstoppable team!"

The first team called up is a man with a golden retriever.

"May I introduce Thomas Castle and his guide dog, Sierra!" the speaker says.

My ears perk up.

Sierra! That's my sister. I'm glad another pup from our litter is a guide dog!

Two more dogs and their owners come

forward and receive certificates.

Finally, Jessie and I are called to the podium.

"I've saved this team for last because Jessie shared some news with us," the speaker says. "Yesterday, Jessie and Sammy were in a café when a fire broke out."

I hear a few murmurs of concern from the audience.

"Working together, they made it out of the building safely. Let's give them an extra round of applause!"

We stand in front while people clap and cheer for us.

After the ceremony, our friends and family gather to congratulate Jessie and me. "May I take a picture for our guide dog newsletter?" a photographer asks.

"Sure!" says Jessie. All the humans from my

past, my present, and my future crowd together. There's Dad, Jayden, and Marcus. Elena, Mei, and Jessie's parents join us too. And right in the middle, there's Jessie, holding the graduation certificate and hugging me.

"Say 'doggy treat,'" the photographer says as he snaps a portrait with all the humans who mean the most in the world to me.

Jessie gives me one more happy squeeze before she stands up and visits with the others. As I watch her smile and talk, I can tell something has changed. I liked Jessie from the time we first met. But since yesterday, we've become closer than ever. I guess that's what happens when you share a few big adventures, some quiet time—and a really great game of catch.

It's been a long road to get here, but we're a real team now, Jessie and me. I know she has big, exciting plans for her future. There will be more for us to learn, and challenges along the way too. But Jessie and I care about each other,

and most importantly, we trust each other.

I know that whatever lies ahead, we're ready to navigate it together.

Dogs have been companions and helpers to humans since ancient times—and this includes faithful canines that serve as guide dogs. In fact, the earliest evidence of a guide dog appears in a mural in Italy that dates back to the first century!

In more recent history, dogs were trained by a German doctor during World War I to help returning soldiers who were blind or had limited vision. The doctor established the first guide dog training school, and since then the number of guide dogs has increased across every decade.

According to the organization Guiding Eyes for the Blind, about 10,000 people in the United States who are blind or visually impaired are partnered with guide dogs. Others may choose to travel with white canes or with sighted guides. Just like Jessie, each person must decide what works best for them.

A trained guide dog can analyze situations and give their human teammate information about their surroundings. But a guide dog is a not GPS device—they cannot tell someone where to go. Instead, a person sets the course, and the dog helps get them to their destination by indicating features to navigate along the way, such as stairs, curbs, and crosswalks. A guide dog is also trained to alert to things they can easily walk under—such as tree branches or low-hanging signs—that might pose problems to their taller human teammate.

Because of the vital work they do, guide dogs are allowed into many places other dogs are not. You might see them in the grocery store or at a restaurant. But no matter where you come across these working dogs, keep in mind that they have important jobs to do. Always remember to ask permission before touching or interacting with a harnessed guide dog.

A guide dog's day is not all work though! Just like other pups, they like to have fun too. When the harness comes off, guide dogs are free to run and sniff, play and explore. Playtime not only helps build the bond between the human and guide dog, it helps ensure that these dedicated working dogs live long, healthy, and happy lives.

Becoming a guide dog is not for all dogs. On the job, a single serious mistake could spell disaster. Because of this, guide dogs must go through months of training before they officially become part of a guide dog team.

At about eight weeks old, potential guide dog pups go to live in homes with volunteer puppy raisers. There they are taught obedience skills and learn to become comfortable around people. At twelve to eighteen months, the dogs return to the training facility. During this "doggy college" time, they develop one of their most important skills: intelligent disobedience. For people-pleasing puppies, learning to disobey in possibly dangerous situations can take months to master.

After passing this stage, each dog is carefully paired with a person who is blind or has a visual impairment, and they begin to form a bond through training, working, and playing together. It's only after a successful pairing that the dogs graduate and become guide dogs. Only about seventy-five percent of dogs that enter guide dog programs complete the training. Others go on to different jobs or are adopted as pets.

Golden Retriever

The golden retriever was first bred as a hunting dog to navigate the rocky terrain of the Scottish Highlands. Today, these beautiful animals make wonderful guide dogs and companions.

Height: 21.5–24 inches
Weight: 55–75 pounds
Life Span: 10–12 years
Coat: Golden, cream
Known for: Kindness, reliability, confidence

Labrador Retriever

Labs were first bred to retrieve ducks from the water. Today, their alertness and friendliness make them excellent guide dogs.

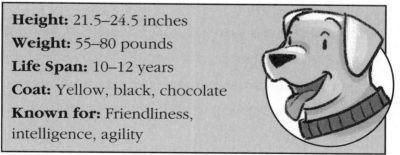

Height: 21.5–24.5 inches
Weight: 55–80 pounds
Life Span: 10–12 years
Coat: Yellow, black, chocolate
Known for: Friendliness, intelligence, agility

Breed information based on American Kennel Club data. For more on these and other breeds, visit www.akc.org/dog-breeds/.

Acknowledgments

On a bright December afternoon, I was welcomed to the Guide Dogs of Texas facility in San Antonio. There I met Jamie Massey, a guide dog mobility instructor and director of training, who answered my many questions and generously shared her expertise—I learned so much from her and am extremely grateful. Later, Ms. Massey kindly answered my follow-up questions and reviewed the manuscript. On that December day, I also met two guide dogs in training, a golden retriever, Hudson, and a yellow Labrador, Indie. Much thanks to Amy Zamora, apprentice guide dog mobility instructor, who showed with Indie the impressive ways guide dogs alert humans to possible hazards such as stairs and low branches.

Thank you, too, to Janell McMullan, educator and Guide Dogs for the Blind leader. Ms. McMullan runs San Antonio's Madison High School Guide Dog Club. In this program, students become puppy raisers and bring their guide-dog-in-training puppies to school each day. Ms. McMullan graciously allowed me to interview her about guide dogs in general, and the experiences of the puppies training in a high school setting.